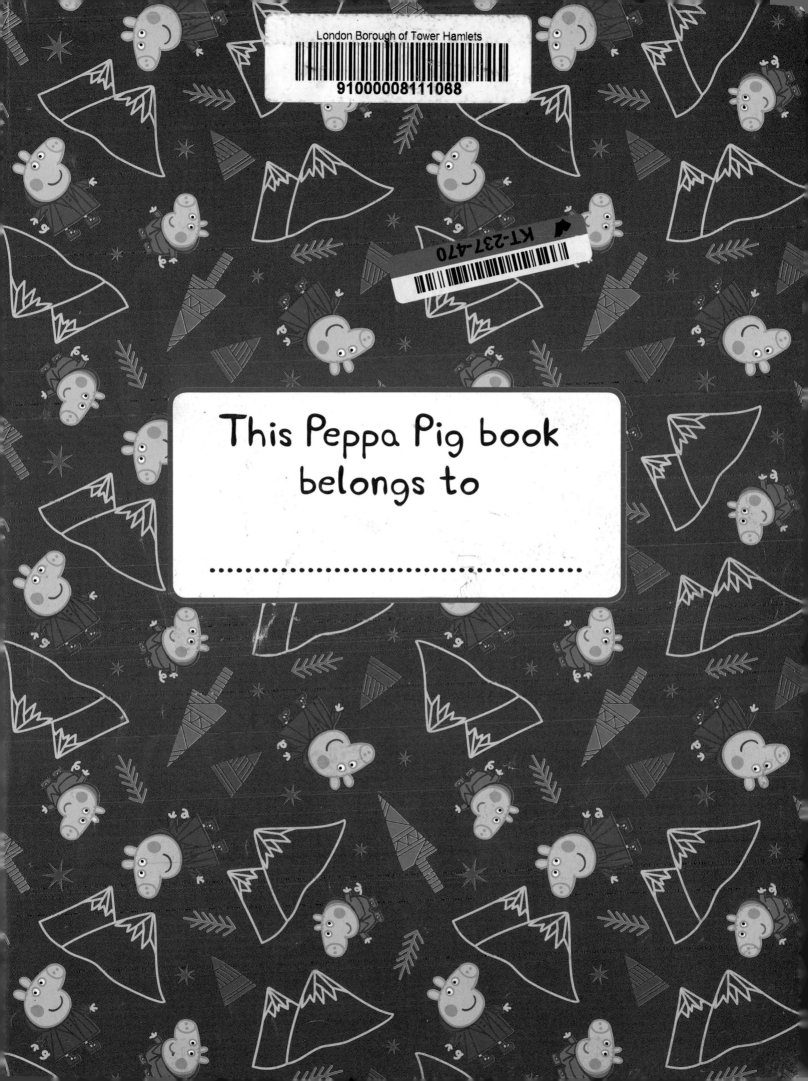

This Peppa Pig book
belongs to

....

LADYBIRD BOOKS

UK | USA | Canada | Ireland | Australia | India | New Zealand | South Africa

Ladybird Books is part of the Penguin Random House group of companies
whose addresses can be found at global.penguinrandomhouse.com.

www.penguin.co.uk   www.puffin.co.uk   www.ladybird.co.uk

Penguin
Random House
UK

First published 2021
001

Licensed by

Printed in China

The authorized representative in the EEA is Penguin Random House Ireland,
Morrison Chambers, 32 Nassau Street, Dublin D02 YH68

A CIP catalogue record for this book is available from the British Library

ISBN: 978-0-241-47676-5

All correspondence to:
Ladybird Books, Penguin Random House Children's
One Embassy Gardens, 8 Viaduct Gardens, London SW11 7BW

Contents

Hooray for Snow Days!

Hip hip hooray – it's a snow day! Join in the winter fun with Peppa and her family!

Snow-Dino

George has been busy building something very special in the snow – a dinosaur! Can you draw a circle around the snowman that looks like a dinosaur? *GRRR!*

Guess Who?

Oh dear! There's been a snowstorm! Draw a line linking each person to the picture of them covered in snow!

Giant Gingerbread

Yummy! Peppa and George are decorating a giant gingerbread house for the Christmas holidays. Can you help them by colouring it in?

Which bit would you eat first?

christmas

8

Snowman Faces

Make some fun paper-plate snowman faces to put on your wall.

You will need: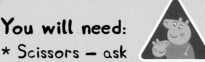
* Scissors — ask a grown-up to help!
* Paper plate
* White tissue paper or cotton-wool balls
* PVA glue
* Orange felt or card
* Black buttons
* Black and coloured card or sugar paper

Hat cut from green card or sugar paper

Green card scarf

How to make:

1 Glue balls of cotton wool or scrunched-up balls of white tissue paper all over your paper plate.

2 Glue on a piece of orange card or felt, cut into a triangle, for the snowman's nose.

3 Add two black button eyes and a mouth of glued-on buttons or card circles.

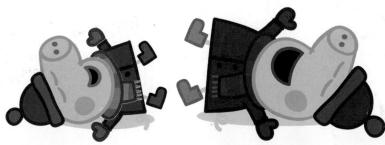

9

Story  Time

Snowy Mountain

Peppa and her family have come to the mountains to go skiing.
The ski-lift is there to carry everyone to the top of Snowy Mountain.
"Er . . . it looks a bit high." says Daddy Pig nervously. Daddy Pig does not like heights.

They get into the ski-lift chairs, and the safety bars come down. *CLANG!*
"*Whoaaaaaa!*" shouts Daddy Pig as they are lifted up into the air.
"This is really fun!" cries Peppa.
"Oh yes," says Daddy Pig. "Really fun!"

"*In the air, in a chair!*" sings Peppa again and again.
The ski lift soon reaches the top of Snowy Mountain. Daddy Pig isn't sure how to get out of the chair . . .
"Oops!" he shouts, falling out of the lift and into the snow. *SPLAT!*

When Peppa, George and Mummy Pig reach the top of the mountain, they find Daddy Pig totally covered in snow!
"Daddy is a walking, talking snowman!" says Peppa, giggling.
"*Brrrrrr!*" says Daddy Pig, shaking off all the snow.

"Skis! Skis! Get your skis here!" calls Miss Rabbit from her ski hut.

"Hello," says Mummy Pig. "Skis for two grown-ups and two children, please."

"There you go," says Miss Rabbit, handing over the skis.

"Yippee!" says Peppa.

Madame Gazelle is Peppa and George's ski teacher.

"Will we ski all the way down the mountain?" asks Peppa.

"Not today, Peppa," says Madame Gazelle. "We'll stick to the baby slope.
To start, push off slowly with your sticks. To stop, point your skis together."

The children copy Madame Gazelle. *Swish, swoosh!*

When they reach the bottom, Madame Gazelle shows the children the gold cup she won for being a World Champion at skiing. The children are very impressed.
"Can we see you do some more skiing?" asks Peppa "*Pleeeeeease!*"
"Very well," says Madame Gazelle.

Wheeee!

Madame Gazelle performs a ski routine with twists, turns and a big jump!
"Ooooh!" gasp the children.
"That was amazing!" says Daddy Pig.
"Yes, well I was the World Champion," says Madame Gazelle. "Now, which mummy or daddy would like a go?"

"Why not?" says Mummy Pig.

"Are you sure, Mummy Pig?" says Daddy Pig. "You haven't skied for years!"

"It's like riding a bike," says Mummy Pig. "You never forget! Which way does this go?"

"All the way down the mountain!" says Madame Gazelle.

Mummy Pig sets off. "Er, where are the brakes?" she says to herself.

WHOOOOOOSH!

Mummy Pig zooms down the mountain very quickly and on to the street below! "Whoaaaaaa! Stand back!" she shouts.

"Wow! My mummy is skiing super fast!" says Peppa, watching from the top of the mountain. "And she did a loop the loop!"

"She can't stop!" says Madame Gazelle. "We have to catch up with her!"

Mummy Pig isn't sure how she is going to stop, but then she hits a big bank of snow . . . *THUMP!*
Everyone skis down to find her at the bottom of the mountain.
"*Mmmmmbbmmb!*" says Mummy Pig through the snow.
"My goodness! A walking, talking snowman!" says Madame Gazelle.
"No, it's just my mummy!" says Peppa.

Mummy Pig shakes off all the snow.
"I have never seen such amazing skiing!" says Madame Gazelle. "This cup belongs to you." Madame Gazelle gives Mummy Pig her World Champion Skier's cup.
"My mummy is the best at skiing down the mountain!" says Peppa.
Everyone laughs. "Hee! Hee! Hee!"

What Comes Next?

Peppa and George love visiting the mountains. Look closely at the patterns below. Can you figure out what comes next in each row?

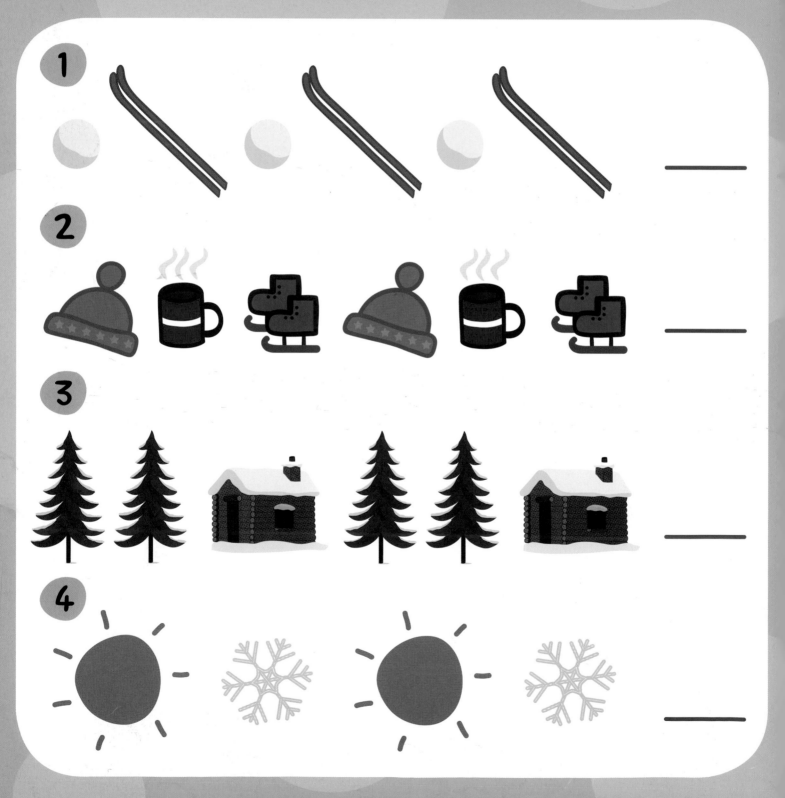

Skiing Search

Skiing is so much fun! Help Peppa and Daddy Pig find Mummy Pig and George so they can all ski together!

How many flags can you see?

Sea Treasure

Peppa and George have found some sea treasure washed up on the beach! Draw lines to sort the treasure into matching pairs. Which thing is the odd one out?

All About Peppa

This page is all about Peppa! Spend a few minutes looking at the pictures, then turn the page to see how much you remember!

This is Peppa Pig.

4

She is 4 years old.

This is Teddy, Peppa's favourite toy.

Peppa's brother is called George.

Peppa's favourite thing to do is jump in muddy puddles. **SPLASH!**

All About Peppa
Memory Quiz

Circle the answers with a pencil or pen.

1. How old is Peppa?
   - a) 3
   - b) 4
   - c) 5

2. Who is Peppa's brother?

3. Which toy is Peppa's favourite?

4. What is Peppa's favourite thing to do?

Answers: 1. b, 2. c, 3. a, 4. b

Cheese Shapes

Colour in each shape as you find it in the picture!

21

Story  Time
The Tall Tree

Peppa and her family are visiting Madame Gazelle at her home.
"Hello, everyone," says Madame Gazelle, opening her creaky door. "Come in!"
"Hello, Madame Gazelle," says Peppa.

As they step into the house, Peppa and George find themselves
sliding down Madame Gazelle's hallway!
"Wheeeeee!" cries Peppa. "Your hallway is a big slide!"
"Hmm. Is it meant to be like that?" asks Daddy Pig.
"No," says Madame Gazelle. "The house is just old."

In the living room, lots of things are leaning to one side.
"Everything here is a little bit wonky!" Peppa gasps.
"Madame Gazelle, I think your house might need fixing," says Daddy Pig.
He peers out through the window and spots a tree pushing against the wall.

Madame Gazelle takes them outside. "It's my little Christmas tree from a long time ago," she explains. "I didn't want to throw it away, so I planted it in the garden."
"Your little tree has grown so much it's pushing your house over!" says Daddy Pig.
"I'll call Mr Bull to see if he can help."

"That's a mighty fine tree you have there, Madame Gazelle," says Mr Bull when he arrives. "Strong roots!"
"Yes," says Daddy Pig. "But it's pushing the house over."
Mr Bull stands back to take a look. "Oh yes," he says. "Let's chop it down!"

Tweet!
Tweet!
Tweet!

Before Mr Bull chops the tree down, he must check that no animals are living it.
He gets a rope and a harness and uses them to climb the tree.
"Look at that!" says Mr Bull. "Little birds are nesting in your tree, Madame Gazelle!"
Peppa, George and Madame Gazelle go and see the birds from the window.

Mr Bull climbs higher up the tree. *Clomp! Clomp! Clomp!*
Peppa, George and Madame Gazelle climb up higher in the house.
"Look what's here!" says Mr Bull.
"Buzzy bees!" cries Peppa. "*Buzzzzz!*"
"Let's see what else there is," says Mr Bull.

Mr Bull climbs higher up the tree. *Clomp! Clomp! Clomp!*
Peppa, George and Madame Gazelle climb the stairs to the third-floor window.
"I say, look at this," whispers Mr Bull.
"It's an owl," Peppa gasps.
"*Twoo!*" says the owl.

"Onward and upward!" says Mr Bull, continuing to climb. *Clomp! Clomp! Clomp!*
Peppa, George and Madame Gazelle reach the highest window in the house.
"Bats!" says Mr Bull, spotting some hanging upside down and fast asleep.
"Ahh, my friends the bats," says Madame Gazelle. "They remind me of the old country . . ."

Mr Bull reaches up. "But what's this?" he asks, pulling down a piece
of tinsel with a bauble on the end.
"Ah! My Christmas decorations!" says Madame Gazelle.
Mr Bull pulls himself right to the very top of the tall tree and finds . . .
"A Christmas fairy!" he cries.

Everyone agrees that, since Madame Gazelle's tree is a wonderful home to so many little animals, it should not be chopped down.
"Maybe to stop your house falling over, we could put it in the tree!" says Daddy Pig.
Mr Bull uses his crane to lift up Madame Gazelle's house . . .

Squeak! Squeak!

Twoo!

Buzzz!

Tweet! Tweet!

. . . and puts it in the middle of the tree!
"I've always wanted a tree house!" gasps Madame Gazelle. "Thank you, everyone!"
All the animals love living in the tall tree. Madame Gazelle loves living in the tall tree!

Wonky House

Look at the two pictures of Madame Gazelle's wonky house. Can you spot five differences between them?

Colour in a tree as you spot each difference.

Tall, Taller, Tallest!

Madame Gazelle's tree grew very tall! Look at these four groups of different things. Can you point to or draw a circle around the tallest thing in each group?

1
a b c d

2
a b c d

Who is the tallest in your family or group of friends?

3
a b c d

4
a b c d

Building Things Up . . .

. . . and knocking them down! Peppa is busy building walls with blocks. Can you help her finish these walls before she knocks them down?

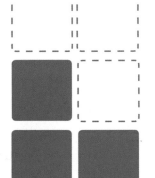

a Peppa has 5 blocks. Draw 1 more block to finish her wall.

b Peppa has 4 blocks. Draw 2 more blocks to finish her wall.

c Peppa has 3 blocks. Draw 3 more blocks to finish her wall.

d Peppa has 2 blocks. Draw 4 more blocks to finish her wall.

Digger Dot-to-Dot

VVVRRRMMM! Mr Rhino is driving a digger! Join the dots to finish the digger below, and then draw what you think Mr Rhino is digging!

Use your pens or pencils to colour in the picture.

Whose Home?

Hoot! Buzz! Squeak! Can you draw lines matching each animal to its home?

1

a

2

b

3

c

4

5

6

d

e

f

Pretend to be one of the animals, and see if a grown-up can guess which one you are!

Sunflower Height Chart

Measure how tall you are growing on a giant sunflower height chart!

How to make:

1. Paint a big sunflower with a long green stem on a sheet of lining paper and fix it to the wall.

2. Cut out some big green sunflower leaves.

3. Measure everyone's height against the sunflower stem and make marks on the paper.

4. Write each person's name on a leaf and stick it on to the sunflower stem to show how tall they are.

5. Measure everyone's height again in a few months' time to see how much they have grown!

You will need:
* Scissors – ask a grown-up to help!
* Long sheet of paper, such as wallpaper lining paper
* Paints
* Paintbrush
* Green card or paper
* Reusable adhesive putty

Daddy Pig

Mummy Pig

Peppa

George

Handprint Trees

Use your hand to print some colourful trees!

You will need:
* Paper
* Paint
* Big paintbrush
* Your hand!
* A sponge

Paint your hand with brown paint and press it on to a sheet of paper to make the tree's trunk and branches.

Dab on blobs of paint with a big brush, a sponge or your fingertips to give your tree pink blossom, green leaves or orange and gold autumn colours.

Jungle Adventure

Shhh! Peppa and George need to be quiet so they can spot lots of amazing creatures in the jungle. Look closely at the big picture, then answer the questions to help Peppa and George with their animal-spotting adventure!

1. How many pink birds are there in the big picture?

2. How many yellow monkeys are there in the big picture?

3. How many orange butterflies are there in the big picture?

4. How many red butterflies are there in the big picture?

5. How many purple monkeys are there in the big picture?

1 2 3 4 5

Answers: 1. three pink birds, 2. one yellow monkey, 3. two orange butterflies, 4. five red butterflies, 5. four purple monkeys

Ballerina Buddies

Peppa and her friends love dressing up and twirling around like ballerinas! Help them get ready by using the numbers to colour in their beautiful ballet costumes.

Fun-tastic Plane Ride!

Peppa and George are off on a fun adventure with Granny and Grandpa Pig. Only one path leads all the way to an exciting place! Can you follow the right path to find out where that place is?

1   **2**   **3**

Answer: Path 2 leads to the exciting place . . . Miss Rabbit's ice-cream stall!

Magical Bingo

Peppa loves fairies . . . and lots of other magical things! Play this game with a friend to see who can collect all the magical things on their card first.

How to play:

1. Ask a grown-up to cut out the magical picture squares on the opposite page, mix them up and place the squares face down in a pile. Next, ask your grown-up to cut out the player cards.

2. Find a friend to play with. Each player should choose a card!

3. Take it in turns to pick up a picture square. If the picture matches one on your player card, place it on top of it. If it doesn't match, put the square back at the bottom of the pile and let the other player take a turn.

4. The first player to fill their card and shout "Magical Bingo!" is the winner.

Player 1

Player 2

41

Lounge Bop!

Peppa and her family love singing and dancing! Grab your favourite colouring pens or pencils and colour in the big picture. You can use the little picture for help . . . or choose your own colours!

What is your favourite type of dancing?

Game, Set, Match!

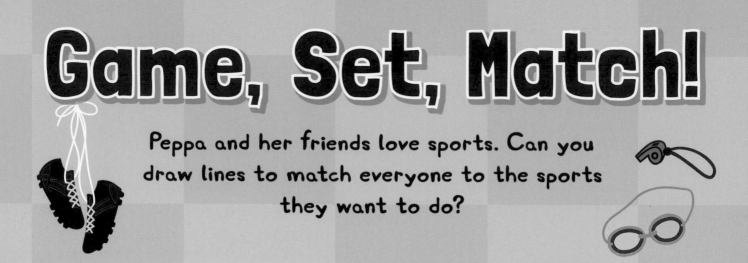

Peppa and her friends love sports. Can you draw lines to match everyone to the sports they want to do?

1

a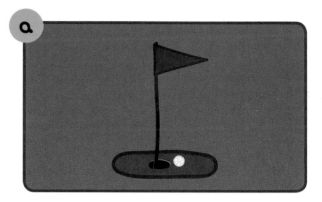

2

b

3

c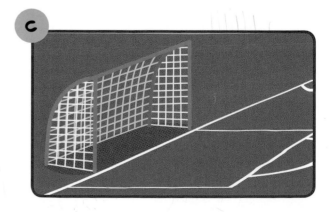

Do you like to do any of these sports? Which one is your favourite?

4

5

6

d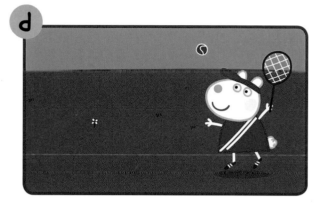

e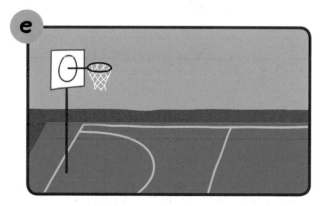

f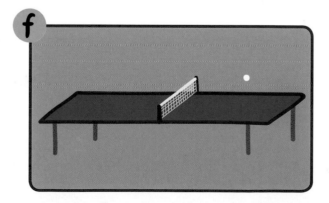

Story  Time

Wendy Wolf's Birthday

Today is Wendy Wolf's birthday, and she has invited all her friends to her party.
"Happy birthday, Wendy!" her friends cheer.
"Thank you, everybody!" says Wendy.

Mr Wolf is blowing up the balloons for the party. "I'll huff and I'll puff
and I'll . . . blow these balloons up! *Pfffft!*"
He blows up lots and lots of balloons and bounces them over for the
children to play with.

"I love balloons!" cries Peppa, bouncing a red one up into the air. *Boink!*
"Me, too!" says Wendy. *Boink! Boink!*
"And me! And me!" everyone agrees.
"Let's try and keep them in the air!" says Freddy Fox. *Boink! Boink! Boink!*

When the children have finished with the balloons, Mrs Wolf asks, "Who wants to play with bubbles?"
"Me! Me! Me!" everyone cheers.
"OK," says Mrs Wolf. "I'll huff and I'll puff and I'll . . . blow some bubbles! *Pfffft!*"
Lots of bubbles float around and the children try to pop them. *Pop! Pop! Pop!*

"Oh," sighs Peppa. "We've popped all the bubbles!"
"We can always make more," says Mrs Wolf. "Who wants a go?"
"Me! Me! Me!" cry the children.
Mrs Wolf hands everyone bubble mixture and tells them to huff, puff and blow!

The bubbles float all the way up into the sky.
"Look at that big bubble!" says Pedro Pony, pointing. All the children look up.
"That's not a bubble, Pedro. That's the full moon!" says Wendy. "When we wolves
see one, we howl . . . *Aooooh!*"

"Can you teach us how to do that, Wendy?" asks Peppa.
"OK," replies Wendy. "First, you look up at the moon . . . then, you howl! *Aooooooooh!*"
Wendy's friends look at the moon. "*Aooooooh!*" they howl.
When they finish, they hear another howl. "*AOOOOH!*"
"Who was that?" gasps Peppa.

The children hear the howl again and huddle together, until . . .
Wendy's granny, Granny Wolf, pops out from the bushes.
"Oh! Hello, Granny!" says Wendy.
"Happy birthday, Wendy!" cries Granny Wolf. "And hello, Wendy's friends!"
"Hello, Granny Wolf," say Wendy's friends quietly.

"My, what big ears you've got, Granny Wolf," says Peppa.
"All the better to hear you with!" replies Granny Wolf.
"What big eyes you've got, Granny Wolf," says Zoe Zebra.
"All the better to see you with!" replies Granny Wolf.

"And what big teeth you've got, Granny Wolf!" says Pedro.
"All the better to eat . . . birthday cake!" replies Granny Wolf, laughing.
"Hooray!" cheer all the children, looking at the lovely birthday cake
Granny Wolf has brought for Wendy.

"Wendy," says Peppa. "What's that on top of your cake?"

"It's a little house made of sticks," says Wendy.

Mrs Wolf tells Wendy it's time to blow out the candles.

"I'll huff and I'll puff and I'll blow the candles out! *Pffffft!*"

Wendy blows the candles out . . . and blows the stick house down, too!

"That's my girl!" says Mrs Wolf, and then she turns to Daddy Pig. "What's your house made of, Mr Pig?"

"Bricks!" replies Daddy Pig.

"Oh, of course," she says.

"That was my best party ever! Thank you!" cheers Wendy Wolf. "*Aoooooh!*"

"*Aooooh!*" everyone howls. "Happy birthday!"

Story Quiz

What do you remember from the story *Wendy Wolf's Birthday*?
Draw circles around the answers, or point to them.

1. Whose birthday was it?

a b c

2. Which two things did the children play with at Wendy's party?

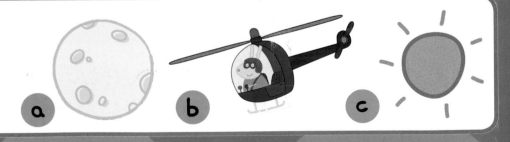

a b c

3. What did Wendy see in the sky to make her howl?

a b c

4. What did Wendy Wolf's cake look like?

a b c

Answers: 1. b, 2. a and b, 3. a, 4. b

Dream Cake

Wendy loves her birthday cake! What would you like on your cake? Use your brightest pens or pencils to decorate your very own delicious dream cake.

What colour icing does it have?

Does it have candles?

Does it have sprinkles?

What flavour is it? Chocolate? Lemon? Carrot?

53

Noisy Party Game

Play Wendy Wolf's noisy party game
and you'll soon be howling with laughter!

How to play:

1. Find some counters, a dice and a friend to play with.

2. Take turns to roll the dice and move your counter
   the number of spaces shown.

   • If you land on a balloon,
     shout *"BOINK!"* and bounce
     on one space.

   • If you land on a bubble,
     blow *"Pfffft!"*, then shout
     "POP!" and move back one space.

   • If you land on a moon howl *"AOOOH!"*
     and move on two spaces!

3. The player who makes it to the finish first can blow
   out all the candles on the birthday cake! Hooray!

Start

Finish

Jigsaw Card

Peppa is making a jigsaw card for Suzy Sheep's birthday! You can make this, too!

How to make:

1 Cut the cardboard into a square measuring 15cm x 15cm.

2 Draw or paint a colourful picture on one side of the cardboard.

3 Draw the outline of a flower, heart or star in thick black felt-tip pen on the other side of the card. Write your message inside the black outline.

4 Using a ruler and pencil, divide the cardboard into 9 squares, then cut along the lines.

Your friend will have to do the jigsaw to read your message!

Post the jigsaw pieces in an envelope.

Pop-up Birdie Card

This birdie card has a surprise
inside – a birdie with a pop-up beak!

How to make:

You will need:
* Scissors – ask a
  grown-up to help!
* Orange, yellow
  and pink card
* PVA glue
* Googly eyes
* Feathers
* Felt-tip pens

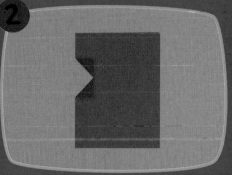

1 Fold a piece of orange card in
half and cut a slit across the
fold, as shown.

2 Fold back the flaps, then push
the folded flaps inside your
card to make the beak.

3 Glue a pink piece of card (the
same size as the orange piece)
behind the orange card, taking
care not to stick it to the beak.

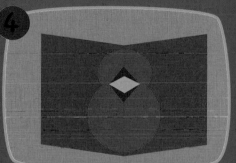

4 Cut out a curved shape from yellow
card for the bird's head and body. Ask
a grown-up to cut a diamond shape
to fit the beak through. Stick it inside
the card.

Glue on some googly
eyes and bright
colourful feathers!

Don't glue the
pink card behind
the beak or the
bird's mouth
won't open!

Decorate the
front of the card
with words or any
design you like!

The flaps open like a beak
when you open the card!

57

Hide-and-Seek

Peppa and George are playing hide-and-seek. George is hiding and Peppa is seeking! Can you find George hiding in all these pictures?

Where would you hide
if you were playing?

What Should Peppa Take?

Yippee! Peppa is going camping and she's very excited! Help her pack by colouring in all the things she needs for her trip.